MR. TALL

by Roger Hargreaves

TO:

_____

FROM:

_____

EAN

ISBN 978-0-8431-7510-3

9 780843 175103

5 0 3 9 9 >

MR. TALL

by Roger Hargreaves

PSS!

PRICE STERN SLOAN

An Imprint of Penguin Group (USA) Inc.

Mr. Tall was very very very tall.

Quite the tallest person you've ever met.

In fact, quite the tallest person you've never met, because you've never met anybody with legs as long as Mr. Tall's legs.

Have you?

Now, the problem with being as tall as Mr. Tall was that life was just one long problem.

As you can see!

"Oh, dear," he used to sigh. "Oh, dear me! I do so wish that my legs weren't quite so very very very long."

He decided to go for a walk to think over his problem.

He was just stepping over a tree when he heard a voice.

A little voice.

"Hello!"

It was Mr. Small, standing underneath a daisy.

But Mr. Tall was so tall he couldn't see him.

So Mr. Small shouted at the top of his voice.

"Hello!"

A Mr. Small shout is about as loud as a bee's sneeze.

So, it took quite some time for Mr. Tall to spot him.

"Oh," he said gloomily, "it's you."

"You don't look very happy," said Mr. Small. "What's up?"

"I am," replied Mr. Tall. "Because of these silly long legs of mine."

"Oh," said Mr. Small.

Mr. Small decided to cheer him up.

"Let's go for a walk together," he suggested.

So they did, which of course didn't work.

It was like a giraffe going for a walk with a mouse!

Then Mr. Small had an idea.

Which did work!

And, because of the length of Mr. Tall's legs, they very quickly walked all the way to the beach.

"Come for a swim," cried Mr. Small.

"Can't," replied Mr. Tall. "By the time I start to swim, I will have reached the other side."

So Mr. Small went for a swim while Mr. Tall sat down with a face which was nearly as long as his legs.

Mr. Tickle came along.

"Hello," he said. "You look as if you need cheering up. Care for a tickle?"

"No thanks," replied Mr. Tall. "What I would care for are some different legs. Mine are much too long."

"So are my arms," said Mr. Tickle cheerfully.
"But all the better for tickling!"

And off he went, chuckling, looking for somebody to tickle.

Looking for anybody to tickle!

Mr. Nosey came along.

"Cheer up," he said. "You look very down in the dumps. What's the problem?"

"It's my legs," replied Mr. Tall. "They're too long!"

"So's my nose," replied Mr. Nosey laughing. "But all the better for poking into other people's business!"

And off he went, looking for something to be nosey about.

Looking for anything to be nosey about.

Mr. Greedy came along.

"Hello," he cried. "You look gloomy! What's wrong?"

"It's my legs," explained Mr. Tall. "They're too big!"

"So is my tummy," replied Mr. Greedy. "But all the better for filling with food!"

And off he went, licking his lips.

Mr. Tall sat there and thought about Mr. Tickle's arms, and Mr. Nosey's nose, and Mr. Greedy's tummy.

He smiled.

And then he grinned.

And then he laughed out loud.

He looked at his legs, those very very very long legs of his.

"All the better for walking," he chuckled.

And walked home.

In four minutes.

Forty miles!

Mr. Small came out of the ocean after his short swim.

"And how am I going to get home?" he asked himself.

So he started walking.

All the way home.

Forty miles!

That was last year.

He got home yesterday!

MR. MEN LITTLE MISS

PRICE STERN SLOAN

SBN 978-0-8431-7510-3

18 17 16 15 14 13 12 11